Nate
the
Great
goes
Undercover

Nate the Great goes Undercover

by
Marjorie Weinman Sharmat
illustrations by Marc Simont

A Yearling Book

Published by
Bantam Doubleday Dell Books for Young Readers
a division of
Bantam Doubleday Dell Publishing Group, Inc.
1540 Broadway
New York, New York 10036

ISBN: 0-440-46302-5

Reprinted by arrangement with Coward, McCann, & Geoghegan, Inc.
Printed in the United States of America

March 1984

50 49 48 47 46 45 44 43

UPR

For my wonderful father, Nate

I,Nate the Great, am a detective.
I work hard,
I rest hard.
Tonight I am resting hard
from my last case.

It was my first night case.
It started in the morning
before breakfast.
I was walking my dog, Sludge.
Sludge is my new dog.
I found him in a field
eating a stale pancake.
I love pancakes.
I knew he was my kind of dog.

I saw Oliver come
out of his house.
Oliver lives next door.
Sludge and I walked faster.
Oliver walked faster.
Oliver caught up with us.
He always catches up with us.
Oliver is a pest.

"There is a garbage snatcher
in the neighborhood," Oliver said.
"Our can is tipped over
every night.
I need help."
Oliver knows I am a detective.
He knows I am a good detective.

"I will help you," I said.
"I, Nate the Great,
will help you
pick up your garbage."
"That is not the kind of help
I need," Oliver said.
"I want to know who is taking
the garbage every night."

"That is easy," I said.
"Somebody hungry
is taking your garbage.
Somebody very hungry.
And sleepy.
Somebody sleepy
from getting up every night
to take your garbage."
"Do you know anybody
hungry and sleepy?" Oliver asked.
"Yes," I said. "Me.
I will find the garbage snatcher
after I eat breakfast."
Sludge and I went home.
I cooked a giant pancake.
I gave some to Sludge.

Then we went outside.
I said to Sludge,
"I'll ask questions
while you sniff. If you sniff any
garbage smells, let me know."
I saw Rosamond coming
down the street with her cats.

Rosamond did not look
hungry or sleepy.
She looked like she always looks.
Strange.

Sludge sniffed while I spoke.
"Rosamond, do you eat garbage?"
Rosamond said, "There are
two thousand other things
I would eat
before I would eat garbage.
First, I would eat hamburger,
ice cream, candy, pickles, bananas,
potato chips, Krispy Krappies,
relish, doughnuts, spaghetti,
ice cubes, mint leaves. . . ."
Rosamond kept talking.
I did not have time
to hear her list
of two thousand things.
I walked on.

Rosamond was still talking.
"Pretzels, artichokes,
baked beans, chocolate pudding,
vegetable soup, walnuts. . . ."
Rosamond had two thousand
reasons for not
taking Oliver's garbage.
But what about her cats?

I went back to Rosamond.

"Cauliflower, wafers, lamb chops," she said. "Peanuts, egg salad. . . ."

"Excuse me," I said.

"Do your cats eat garbage?"

"No," Rosamond said. "My cats eat cat food, cheese, tuna fish, milk, salmon pie, liver loaf. . . ."

I walked away.

I decided to look for Esmeralda.
Esmeralda always has
her mouth open.
She is either hungry
or about to yawn.
I saw her sitting
in front of her house.
Sludge sniffed. I spoke.
"Do you get up at night to visit
Oliver's garbage can?" I asked.
"I would never visit anything
that belongs to Oliver,"
Esmeralda said.
"He might follow me."
Now I knew why Esmeralda
keeps her mouth open.

She has wise things to say.
She had given me
an important clue.
No person would go near
Oliver or his garbage.
Oliver is too much of a pest.

Sludge and I went home.

Oliver came over.

Oliver always comes over.

Sludge sniffed Oliver.

I gave Sludge a pancake.

"Is the case solved?" Oliver asked.

"Part of it," I said.

"Which part?" he asked.

"I, Nate the Great, have found out

who did *not* take your garbage.
A person did not
take your garbage."
"Well, who took it?" Oliver asked.
"That is the part
that is not solved," I said.
"I, Nate the Great, say
that an animal or bird took it.
An animal or bird that goes out
in the night. I will find out what
and I will be back."
Sometimes I, Nate the Great,
need help.
I went to the library.
I read about birds that
go out in the night.

They are called Strigiformes
and Caprimulgiformes.
I wrote the names down.
Then I crossed them out.
Birds with names like that

would not eat anything
called garbage.
Then I read about cats, rats, bats,
mice, shrews, skunks, raccoons,
opossums, and moles.
They all go out at night.

I read about what they like
and what they do not like.
Then I went home.
Oliver came over.
I said, "A cat, rat, bat, mouse,
shrew, skunk, raccoon, opossum,
or mole is taking your garbage."

"Which one?" Oliver asked.
"I don't know. But tonight,
I, Nate the Great, will find out."
I left a note for my mother.

Dear mother,
I am sleeping out tonight.
I am taking a blanket.
I am taking pancakes.
I will be back.
Love,
Nate the Great

I went out into the yard.

It was cold out there.

I asked Sludge if I could share

his doghouse.

I crawled in.

Sludge crawled out.

It was a small doghouse.
I looked out the window
of the doghouse.
I could not see
Oliver's garbage can.
I crawled out of the doghouse.
I left Sludge a pancake.

Where could I hide?
I, Nate the Great,
knew where to hide.
In the garbage can.
I was sorry I knew.
Detective work is not
fun and games.

Detective work is dirty garbage
cans instead of clean beds.
Detective work is banana peels,
dishrags, milk cartons, floor
sweepings, cigar ashes, fleas,
and me
all together in one can.

I peeked out
from under the cover.
The street was quiet.
Then I heard a sound.
Crunch! Crackle! Klunk!
The sound was close to me.
The sound was me.

The garbage can was crunchy
and crackly and klunky.
Every time I moved
it was crunchier and cracklier.
I lifted up the cover. I got out.
I had a new plan. A better plan.
I would not wait
for the garbage snatcher.
I would go out and find him.

I crept down the street.
I looked to the right
and to the left
and behind me.
Right, left, behind.
Right, left, behind.
Smack!
Something big hit me.
It was in front of me.
The one place I forgot to look.

I do not think
I made a dent
in the telephone pole.
I kept creeping and looking.
Right, left, behind, front.
Right, left, behind, front.
I came to a field.
Animals like fields.
I saw an animal.

I, Nate the Great, was in luck.

I crept closer.

I, Nate the Great, was in bad luck.

It was a skunk.

I started to walk backward.

I saw some stuff on the ground
next to the skunk.

It looked like garbage.

I walked forward to see.

I saw some garbage.

The skunk saw me.

The skunk stamped his feet.

He raised his tail.

I, Nate the Great,

did not run fast enough.

But the case was solved.

The skunk

was the garbage snatcher.

I went home.

I wrote a note to Oliver.

I put it in his mailbox.

Dear Oliver,
I, Nate the great, have found out
who took your garbage.
It was a skunk.
I, Nate the great,
know how to get rid of
a skunk.
Put a can of mothballs
next to your garbage can.
Skunks do not like the smell of
mothballs.
I learned this in the Library.
I do not like the smell of skunks.
I learned this in the field.
Yours truly,
Nate the great

It was not morning yet.
But I knew there was something
I must do
right away.
I was glad the water was hot.
In fact, that is how
I spent most of the next day.

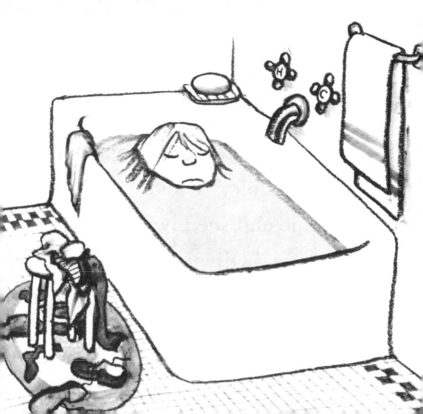

The following morning

Oliver came over.

"The case is unsolved," he said.

"The garbage can is tipped again."

"Impossible," I said.

"Come and see my

garbage," Oliver said.

I, Nate the Great, have had

better invitations.

But I went.

The can was tipped, all right.

"And here is the can of mothballs,"

Oliver said. "So who is

the garbage snatcher?" he asked.

"I, Nate the Great, will find out,

no matter how long

or how many baths it takes."

I walked away.
Sludge followed me.
He was doing a lot of sniffing.
But, I, Nate the Great,
had a lot of thinking to do.
I gave Sludge a pancake.
There must be a clue I missed.
Sludge ignored the pancake.

He was thinking, too.

I thought harder.

And harder.

Then I knew what the clue was.

All I needed was the proof.

I left a note for my mother.

Dear mother,
I will be next door tonight.
I will have a cover.
I will be back.
Love,
Nate the Great

I went to the garbage can.

I stepped inside.

I put the cover over me.

I left space to look out
and to breathe.

I knew that was important.

I waited.

Nothing happened.

Something came up to the can.

Something knocked
the cover to the ground.

Something looked inside.

"Something" was Sludge.
Sludge was surprised to see me.
But, I, Nate the Great, had been
expecting to see Sludge.

I knew that Sludge
was the garbage snatcher.
And I knew why.
Sludge was tired of my pancakes.
How could anybody
be tired of pancakes?
Sludge was looking
for his own snack.
Sludge was hungry.
I took him back to his doghouse.
I gave him a bone
and a bowl of dog food.
Someday Sludge
will be a great detective,
when he learns to sniff more
and snatch less.

I wanted to take a bath.

But I was too tired.

I wanted to write a note to Oliver.

But I was too tired.

Tomorrow Oliver will come over.

Oliver always comes over.

Now I am resting.

I can hear the sounds of the night.
I can hear the sounds of a
crunchy bone being crunched.
They are good sounds.
My first night case is over.
Maybe it will be
my last night case.
I, Nate the Great, am pooped.

Nate The Great

Needs Your Help!

ISBN: 0-385-32601-7

Nate The Great
and me

by Marjorie Weinman Sharmat

illustrated by Marc Simont

The Case of the Fleeing Fang

Includes Detective Tips & Activities!

Join everyone's favorite detective in solving "The Case of the Fleeing Fang." Nate shares his expert detective tips in this fun-filled mystery, which includes recipes, activities, and your very own detective certificate.